Printed in the United States of America.

04 03 02

10 9 8 7 6 5 4 3 2 1

First Printing

2
B
R
O
2
B

by KURT VONNEGUT, JR

Everything was perfectly swell.

There were no prisons, no slums, no insane asylums, no cripples, no poverty, no wars.

All diseases were conquered. So was old age.

Death, barring accidents, was an adventure for volunteers.

The population of the United States was stabilized at forty-million souls.

One bright morning in the Chicago Lying-in Hospital, a man named Edward K. Wehling, Jr., waited for his wife to give birth. He was the only man waiting. Not many people were born a day any more.

Wehling was fifty-six, a mere stripling in a population whose average age was one hundred and twenty-nine.

X-rays had revealed that his wife was going to have triplets. The children would be his first.

Young Wehling was hunched in his chair, his head in his hand. He was so rumpled, so still and colorless as to be virtually invisible. His camouflage was perfect, since the waiting room had a disorderly and demoralized air, too. Chairs and ashtrays had been moved away from the walls. The floor was paved with spattered dropcloths.

1

The room was being redecorated. It was being redecorated as a memorial to a man who had volunteered to die.

A sardonic old man, about two hundred years old, sat on a stepladder, painting a mural he did not like. Back in the days when people aged visibly, his age would have been guessed at thirty-five or so. Aging had touched him that much before the cure for aging was found.

The mural he was working on depicted a very neat garden. Men and women in white, doctors and nurses, turned the soil, planted seedlings, sprayed bugs, spread fertilizer.

Men and women in purple uniforms pulled up weeds, cut down plants that were old and sickly, raked leaves, carried refuse to trash-burners.

Never, never, never—not even in medieval Holland nor old Japan—had a garden been more formal, been better tended. Every plant had all the loam, light, water, air and nourishment it could use.

A hospital orderly came down the corridor, singing under his breath a popular song:

If you don't like my kisses, honey,
Here's what I will do:
I'll go see a girl in purple,
Kiss this sad world toodle-oo.
If you don't want my lovin',
Why should I take up all this space?

I'll get off this old planet,
Let some sweet baby have my place.

The orderly looked in at the mural and the muralist. "Looks so real," he said, "I can practically imagine I'm standing in the middle of it."

"What makes you think you're not in it?" said the painter. He gave a satiric smile. "It's called 'The Happy Garden of Life,' you know."

"That's good of Dr. Hitz," said the orderly.

He was referring to one of the male figures in white, whose head was a portrait of Dr. Benjamin Hitz, the hospital's Chief Obstetrician. Hitz was a blindingly handsome man.

"Lot of faces still to fill in," said the orderly. He meant that the faces of many of the figures in the mural were still blank. All blanks were to be filled with portraits of important people on either the hospital staff or from the Chicago Office of the Federal Bureau of Termination.

"Must be nice to be able to make pictures that look like something," said the orderly.

The painter's face curdled with scorn. "You think I'm proud of this daub?" he said. "You think this is my idea of what life really looks like?"

"What's your idea of what life looks like?" said the orderly.

The painter gestured at a foul dropcloth. "There's a good picture of it," he said. "Frame that, and you'll have a picture a damn sight more honest than this one."

"You're a gloomy old duck, aren't you?" said the orderly.

"Is that a crime?" said the painter.

The orderly shrugged. "If you don't like it here, Grandpa—" he said, and he finished the thought with the trick telephone number that people who didn't want to live any more were supposed to call. The zero in the telephone number he pronounced "naught."

The number was: "2 B R 0 2 B."

It was the telephone number of an institution whose fanciful sobriquets included: "Automat," "Birdland," "Cannery," "Catbox," "De-louser," "Easy-go," "Good-by, Mother," "Happy Hooligan," "Kiss-me-quick," "Lucky Pierre," "Sheepdip," "Waring Blendor," "Weep-no-more" and "Why Worry?"

"To be or not to be" was the telephone number of the municipal gas chambers of the Federal Bureau of Termination.

The painter thumbed his nose at the orderly. "When I decide it's time to go," he said, "it won't be at the Sheepdip."

"A do-it-yourselfer, eh?" said the orderly. "Messy business, Grandpa. Why don't you have a little consideration for the people who have to clean up after you?"

The painter expressed with an obscenity his lack of concern for the tribulations of his survivors. "The world could do with a good deal more mess, if you ask me," he said.

The orderly laughed and moved on.

Wehling, the waiting father, mumbled something without raising his head. And then he fell silent again.

A coarse, formidable woman strode into the waiting room on spike heels. Her shoes, stockings, trench coat, bag and overseas cap were all purple, the purple the painter called "the color of grapes on Judgment Day."

The medallion on her purple musette bag was the seal of the Service Division of the Federal Bureau of Termination, an eagle perched on a turnstile.

The woman had a lot of facial hair—an unmistakable mustache, in fact. A curious thing about gas-chamber hostesses was that, no matter how lovely and feminine they were when recruited, they all sprouted mustaches within five years or so.

"Is this where I'm supposed to come?" she said to the painter.

"A lot would depend on what your business was," he said. "You aren't about to have a baby, are you?"

"They told me I was supposed to pose for some picture," she said. "My name's Leora Duncan." She waited.

"And you dunk people," he said.

"What?" she said.

"Skip it," he said.

"That sure is a beautiful picture," she said. "Looks just like heaven or something."

"Or something," said the painter. He took a list of names from his smock pocket. "Duncan, Duncan, Duncan," he said, scanning the list. "Yes—here you are. You're entitled to be immortalized. See any faceless body here you'd like me to stick your head on? We've got a few choice ones left."

She studied the mural bleakly. "Gee," she said, "they're all the same to me. I don't know anything about art."

"A body's a body, eh?" he said, "All righty. As a master of fine art, I recommend this body here."

He indicated a faceless figure of a woman who was carrying dried stalks to a trash-burner.

"Well," said Leora Duncan, "that's more the disposal people, isn't it? I mean, I'm in service. I don't do any disposing."

The painter clapped his hands in mock delight. "You say you don't know anything about art, and then you prove in the next breath that you know more about it than I do! Of course the sheave-carrier is wrong for a hostess! A snipper, a pruner—that's more your line." He pointed to a figure in purple who was sawing a dead branch from an apple tree. "How about her?" he said. "You like her at all?"

"Gosh—" she said, and she blushed and became humble—"that—that puts me right next to Dr. Hitz."

"That upsets you?" he said.

"Good gravy, no!" she said. "It's—it's just such an honor."

"Ah, You admire him, eh?" he said.

"Who doesn't admire him?" she said, worshiping the portrait of Hitz. It was the portrait of a tanned, white-haired, omnipotent Zeus, two hundred and forty years old. "Who doesn't admire him?" she said again. "He was responsible for setting up the very first gas chamber in Chicago."

"Nothing would please me more," said the painter, "than to put you next to him for all time. Sawing off a limb—that strikes you as appropriate?"

"That is kind of like what I do," she said. She was demure about what she did. What she did was make people comfortable while she killed them.

And, while Leora Duncan was posing for her portrait, into the waitingroom bounded Dr. Hitz himself. He was seven feet tall, and he boomed with importance, accomplishments, and the joy of living.

"Well, Miss Duncan! Miss Duncan!" he said, and he made a joke. "What are you doing here?" he said. "This isn't where the people leave. This is where they come in!"

"We're going to be in the same picture together," she said shyly.

"Good!" said Dr. Hitz heartily. "And, say, isn't that some picture?"

"I sure am honored to be in it with you," she said.

"Let me tell you," he said, "I'm honored to be in it with you. Without women like you, this wonderful world we've got wouldn't be possible."

He saluted her and moved toward the door that led to the delivery rooms. "Guess what was just born," he said.

"I can't," she said.

"Triplets!" he said.

"Triplets!" she said. She was exclaiming over the legal implications of triplets.

The law said that no newborn child could survive unless the parents of the child could find someone who would volunteer to die. Triplets, if they were all to live, called for three volunteers.

"Do the parents have three volunteers?" said Leora Duncan.

"Last I heard," said Dr. Hitz, "they had one, and were trying to scrape another two up."

"I don't think they made it," she said. "Nobody made three appointments with us. Nothing but singles going through today, unless somebody called in after I left. What's the name?"

"Wehling," said the waiting father, sitting up, red-eyed and frowzy. "Edward K. Wehling, Jr., is the name of the happy father-to-be."

He raised his right hand, looked at a spot on the wall, gave a hoarsely wretched chuckle. "Present," he said.

"Oh, Mr. Wehling," said Dr. Hitz, "I didn't see you."

"The invisible man," said Wehling.

"They just phoned me that your triplets have been born," said Dr. Hitz. "They're all fine, and so is the mother. I'm on my way in to see them now."

"Hooray," said Wehling emptily.

"You don't sound very happy," said Dr. Hitz.

"What man in my shoes wouldn't be happy?" said Wehling. He gestured with his hands to symbolize care-free simplicity. "All I have to do is pick out which one of the triplets is going to live, then deliver my maternal grandfather to the Happy Hooligan, and come back here with a receipt."

Dr. Hitz became rather severe with Wehling, towered over him. "You don't believe in population control, Mr. Wehling?" he said.

"I think it's perfectly keen," said Wehling tautly.

"Would you like to go back to the good old days, when the population of the Earth was twenty billion—about to become forty billion, then eighty billion, then one hundred and sixty billion? Do you know what a drupelet is, Mr. Wehling?" said Hitz.

"Nope," said Wehling sulkily.

"A drupelet, Mr. Wehling, is one of the little knobs, one of the little pulpy grains of a blackberry," said Dr. Hitz. "Without population control, human beings would now be packed on this surface of this old planet like drupelets on a blackberry! Think of it!"

Wehling continued to stare at the same spot on the wall.

"In the year 2000," said Dr. Hitz, "before scientists stepped in and laid down the law, there wasn't even enough drinking water to go around, and nothing to eat but sea-weed—and still people insisted on their right to reproduce like jackrabbits. And their right, if possible, to live forever."

"I want those kids," said Wehling quietly. "I want all three of them."

"Of course you do," said Dr. Hitz. "That's only human."

"I don't want my grandfather to die, either," said Wehling.

"Nobody's really happy about taking a close relative to the Catbox," said Dr. Hitz gently, sympathetically.

"I wish people wouldn't call it that," said Leora Duncan.

"What?" said Dr. Hitz.

"I wish people wouldn't call it 'the Catbox,' and things like that," she said. "It gives people the wrong impression."

"You're absolutely right," said Dr. Hitz. "Forgive me." He corrected himself, gave the municipal gas chambers their official title, a title no one ever used in conversation. "I should have said, 'Ethical Suicide Studios,'" he said.

"That Return of the TycoonReturn of the Tycoon.

"This child of yours—whichever one you decide to keep, Mr. Wehling," said Dr. Hitz. "He or she is going to live on a happy, roomy, clean, rich planet, thanks to population control. In a garden like that mural there." He shook his head. "Two centuries ago, when I was a young man, it was a hell that nobody thought could last another twenty years. Now centuries of peace and plenty stretch before us as far as the imagination cares to travel."

He smiled luminously.

The smile faded as he saw that Wehling had just drawn a revolver.

Wehling shot Dr. Hitz dead. "There's room for one— a great big one," he said.

And then he shot Leora Duncan. "It's only death," he said to her as she fell. "There! Room for two."

And then he shot himself, making room for all three of his children.

Nobody came running. Nobody, seemingly, heard the shots.

The painter sat on the top of his stepladder, looking down reflectively on the sorry scene.

The painter pondered the mournful puzzle of life demanding to be born and, once born, demanding to be fruitful ... to multiply and to live as long as possible—to do all that on a very small planet that would have to last forever.

All the answers that the painter could think of were grim. Even grimmer, surely, than a Catbox, a Happy Hooligan, an Easy Go. He thought of war. He thought of plague. He thought of starvation.

He knew that he would never paint again. He let his paintbrush fall to the drop-cloths below. And then he decided he had had about enough of life in the Happy Garden of Life, too, and he came slowly down from the ladder.

He took Wehling's pistol, really intending to shoot himself.

But he didn't have the nerve.

And then he saw the telephone booth in the corner of the room. He went to it, dialed the well-remembered number: "2 B R 0 2 B."

"Federal Bureau of Termination," said the very warm voice of a hostess.

"How soon could I get an appointment?" he asked, speaking very carefully.

"We could probably fit you in late this afternoon, sir," she said. "It might even be earlier, if we get a cancellation."

"All right," said the painter, "fit me in, if you please." And he gave her his name, spelling it out.

"Thank you, sir," said the hostess. "Your city thanks you; your country thanks you; your planet thanks you. But the deepest thanks of all is from future generations."

THE END